D0620715

THIS BLOOMSBURY BOOK

BELONGS TO

....

To Lynne with love - JE
For Marianne, Alex, Rosie and Daniel - DM

First published in Great Britain 1997
by Bloomsbury Publishing PLC
38 Soho Square, London, W1V 5DF
This paperback edition first published 1999

All rights reserved
No part of this publication may be reproduced
or transmitted by any means, electronic, mechanical, photocopying
or otherwise, without the prior permission of the publisher

Copyright © Text Jim Eldridge 1997
Copyright © Illustrations David Melling 1997

Designed by Dave Crook

The moral right of the author and illustrator has been asserted
A CIP catalogue record of this book is available from the
British Library

ISBN 0 7475 3796 8 (paperback)
ISBN 0 7475 3041 6 (hardback)

10 9 8 7 6 5 4 3 2 1

Printed in Hong Kong/China

Tractor and Digger
save the day

Jim Eldridge
Illustrated by David Melling

BLOOMSBURY
CHILDREN'S
BOOKS

'What have you been doing today on the farm?' asked Dougie Digger with a smirk. 'Keeping out of the way of the chickens? Moving manure from one field to another?'

'Oh, this and that,' said Max Tractor. 'We're enjoying the peace and quiet at the moment because soon it'll be silage time. Then there's nothing but work, work, work, for all of us. Even Grandma has to put her shovel in. There's just no rest when it's time to make silage.'

'Silage!' laughed Dougie Digger. 'Yes, that's pretty exciting stuff for you, I guess.' Then he smirked again. 'Do you know what we've been doing today?'

'Building an airport!'

'The whole family of us Diggers will be out there for months and months, moving earth and clearing ground ready for the runways so the aeroplanes can land and take off.' He smiled. 'You ever seen an aeroplane, Max Tractor? They fly around in the sky and travel all over the world!'

'We've got birds that fly around all the time at Runaround Farm,' said Max Tractor. 'And some of them fly all over the world too.'

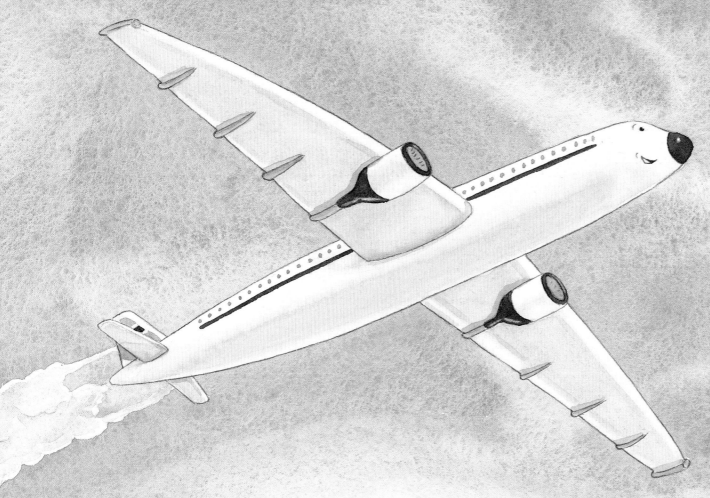

'Huh, birds!' snorted Dougie Digger. 'These planes are big, big, big! So big that you couldn't even fit one in the whole of your old farm, that's how big they are. These planes are so big . . .'

'. . . that they couldn't even fit in your radiator,' snorted Max Tractor.

'Ha! You're jealous!' said Dougie Digger. 'Jealous, jealous, jealous!'

'Me, jealous of you building an airport!' laughed Max Tractor. 'All that dust and muck and all those humans pushing you about?'

Just then Dougie Digger's mother called out, 'Come in, it's diesel time!'

'Coming!' called Dougie Digger. Just before he
went into the contract yard, he grinned again
at Max Tractor and stuck out his starting handle.

'Jealous!' he said again.
Then he drove off, puffing
smoke as he went.

Max Tractor turned on his wheels and drove slowly back up the track. Jealous? Yes, he was! Why did he have to stay here, stuck on the farm, keeping out of the way of the chickens, helping his Dad move manure from one place to another, just like Dougie Digger said?

Max Tractor looked around the farmyard. Oh, to see somewhere different for a change! To be like Dougie Digger: one day building an airport,

the next clearing earth for a motorway,

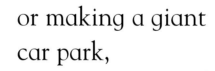

or making a giant car park,

or laying the foundations for a huge building!

Max sighed.

'Don't you sometimes wish you were somewhere else, Grandma?' asked Max Tractor. 'A change from the farm?'

'No,' said Grandma contentedly cleaning her diesel pipe after supper. 'Though, of course, farming isn't what it used to be. Now when I was a young Tractor, before I met your Grandad . . .'

'Oh no, she's off again,' Max Tractor groaned, and he closed his eyes, and went to sleep.

In the contractor yard night was falling. The Diggers looked across the valley at the lights of Runaround Farm.

'Our hillbilly tractor cousins will be settling down for the night,' snickered Uncle Digger. 'Getting the straw out of their engines.'

'But you know,' said Dad Digger, 'it's all very exciting never knowing where you're going to be working from one day to the next, but now and then I think it'd be nice to stay in just one place for a while.'

'With just one person to drive us,' added Mum Digger. 'I get fed up with different people being in charge of us every day. They don't take proper care of us because they know that the next day someone else is going to use us.'

A farm, thought Dougie Digger. With the same person taking care of you every day. He sighed. Maybe Max Tractor was the lucky one after all.

That night it began to rain . . . and rain and rain and
rain and rain.

Up at Runaround Farm, Grandad Tractor said:
'If it doesn't stop raining the river will burst its banks
and ruin all the crops.'

At the contractor yard, Dad Digger said: 'If it doesn't stop raining the river will burst its banks and the town will be flooded and all the people will lose their homes.'

But the rain still came down . . . and the river rose higher and higher.

In the middle of the night the sound of the warning siren tore through the night, waking up the small town, screeching across the farmland. The river was about to burst its banks!

The people hastily put on their clothes and boots and set to work filling sacks with sand and piling them up on the river bank but as fast as they did so, the weight of water pushed the sandbags back.

'We have to build a wall or the town and the farms will drown!' said the Fire Chief. 'We need machines, urgently!'

The machines were already on their way! From Runaround
Farm came Grandad, Grandma, Dad and Mum Tractor, with
Max Tractor hurrying to keep up.

And from the contractor yard came Dad and Mum Digger, and all the other machines, with Dougie Digger steaming along behind them.

Together the machines set to work, their tracks and thick tyres only just keeping a grip as they moved through the mud and rising water, moving earth from here and there, packing it into the banks of the river, and building up a wall of clay and earth and rocks. By dawn the rain had stopped.

'It's working!' shouted the Fire Chief.
'The machines have done it, they've saved us!'

Gradually the surface of the river settled down, lapping against the banks of the wall of earth the machines had created: the Tractors and the Diggers working together.

'That was exciting!' said Dougie Digger.
'It sure was!' grinned Max Tractor.
'Almost as exciting as working on an airport, hey?'

And both Dougie Digger and Max Tractor burst into laughter.

Grandad Tractor looked at them and blinked his headlights in bewilderment.

'What on earth are those two laughing at?' he asked.

'Kids!' sighed Mum Digger.